Nebraska Native Americans

A Kid's Look at Our State's Chiefs, Tribes, Reservations, Powwows, Lore, and M... The Past and the Present

By Carole Marsh

Native American Heritage™

Graphic Design: Lynette Rowe • Cover Design: Victoria DeJoy

Published by
GALLOPADE™ INTERNATIONAL
800-536-2GET
www.gallopade.com

Gallopade is proud to be a member of these educational organizations and associations:

The National School Supply and Equipment Association (NSSEA)
American Booksellers Association (ABA)
Virginia Educational Media Association (VEMA)
Association of Partners for Public Lands (APPL)
Museum Store Association (MSA)
National Association for Gifted Children (NAGC)
Publishers Marketing Association (PMA)
International Reading Association (IRA)
Association of African American Museums (AAAM)

Native American Heritage™ Series

Native American Big Activity Book

Native American Biographies

Native American Coloring Book

Native American Heritage Book

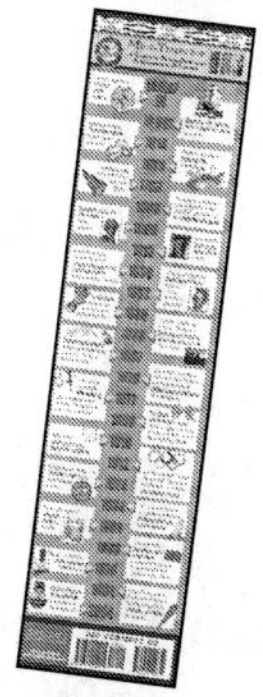

Native American Timeline

Nebraska State Stuff™

My First Pocket Guide: Nebraska
My First Book About Nebraska
Nebraska Coloring Book
The Big Nebraska Reproducible Activity Book
Jeopardy: Answers & Questions About Our State
Nebraska "Jography!": A Fun Run Through Our State
Nebraska Gamebooks
Nebraska Bingo Games
Nebraska Illustrated Timelines
Nebraska Project Books
Nebraska Bulletin Board Set
Nebraska PosterMap
Nebraska Stickers
Let's Discover Nebraska! CD-ROM

Word from the Author

Hello!

I hope you are as interested in North America's wonderful Indian heritage as I am!

Like most kids, I grew up thinking of Indians as the other half of Cowboys. Today, of course, we are getting a much clearer and more accurate picture of what the first peoples on our land were all about. These "facts" are much more fascinating than anything Hollywood can make up. And you probably won't find much of this information in your history textbook!

I am 1/16 Cherokee. This is something I am very proud of and happy about. My grandmother was 1/4 Cherokee. She had tan skin, long gray hair and a very Indian look – especially if I did something bad! Her maiden name was Carrie Corn. Of course, when she got married, she took her husband's name, so it was many years before I learned to appreciate the significance of my native heritage.

Today, I'm trying to make up for lost time by exploring my roots as deeply as I can. One of the most interesting things I've learned is how fascinating all of the Indian tribes are – in the past, the present and future!

As you read about "your" Indians, remember that all native peoples were part of an ever-changing network of time, ideas, power and luck — good and bad. This is certainly a history that is not "dead," but continues to change – often right outside our own back doors! – all the time.

Carole Marsh
She-Who-Writes

PS: Many references show different spellings for the same word. I have tried to select the most common spelling for the time period described. I would not want to be in an Indian spelling bee!

A is for . . .

Archaic Culture

Early peoples who lived in Nebraska from about 5000 B.C. to A.D. 1. Hunted and gathered wild plants.

Awl

An Indian's "needle." Often made from wood, thorns, bone, or metal, it was used to punch holes in skins so they could be sewn together.

Adze

An Indian woodworking tool used to cut, scrape, or gouge; often used to hollow dugout canoes. Blades were made of stone, shell, bone or copper.

Agriculture

Early Nebraska Indians slowly learned to farm. Corn or maize was a staple crop. They used tools like stone axes to clear trees and bowls to grind corn.

Ash Hollow

In 1855, Gen. William Harney and 600 U.S. soldiers defeated the Sioux at this site along the Platte River. Also known as the Battle of Blue Water.

Altar

A platform made of rocks or animal skulls; some had bowls, feathers, rattles, or skins on them. Indians prayed at these altars for things like good crops or expert hunting skills.

Arrow

A long, slender shaft made of reed, cane, or wood; pointed tip was attached to one end and split feathers to the other. Feathers helped the arrows fly straight.

Arrowhead

The pointed tip of an arrow, made of bone, antler, wood, or iron. Some tips had barbs that would embed themselves in flesh. These barbs made it difficult for an enemy to remove the arrowhead from a wound.

Art

The Pawnee and Omaha Indians developed some of the most sophisticated poetry, songs and religious ceremonies of all the Indians of the Great Plains.

Aborigine

A member of the earliest known population of a region.

B is for . . .

Black Bird

Omaha Indian chief, who it was said, was a river pirate who took valuables from every trader who came down the Missouri River. When Lewis and Clark passed his gravesite, they planted an American flag on it.

Band

A subdivision of an Indian tribe. In earlier times, a band was sometimes created when part of a tribe split off from the main group. The band also chose new leadership.

Blankets

Used for door covers, partitions, bags, to dry food on, carry babies and many other purposes.

Baskets

Some were woven and others were coiled. Baskets were made from roots, grasses, barks, and other natural materials.

Buffalo

Made up the major diet of many Nebraska Indian tribes. Hides were used as blankets or tents. Every tribe member was given a piece of the animal to eat. There were strict rules about not hunting buffalo alone, so that one person wouldn't scare them all away! To catch the animals, the hunters chased them off cliffs or encircled them in fire, then shot them.

Buckskin

Softened, smoke-treated rawhide. Used by Nebraska Indians to make clothes, bags and pouches.

Bow

Made from wood, horn or bone. Nebraska Indian children learned how to use bows. The bowstring was made from animal gut, rawhide or twisted vegetable fibers.

Bone

Animal bones were used by Nebraska Indians to make buttons, whistles and other items.

Beads

Made of wood, shells, claws, minerals, seeds — you name it! Later, the Nebraska Indians traded with white men for glass beads, used in some of their decorative arts.

C is for . . .

Chief

Leader of a tribe. Different titles meant different things. Some members were made chief because they owned deeds to land. Chieftainship was often inherited, usually from the mother!

Contact Period

What historians call the era in the 1500s when Native Americans first met Europeans. This meeting changed the lifestyle of the Nebraska Indians more than anyone could ever have anticipated!

Council Bluff

At the site of today's Fort Atkinson. Where explorers Meriwether Lewis and William Clark met with Nebraska's Otoe and Pawnee Indians in 1804. They encouraged the Indians to come under the rule of the "Great Father" in Washington, D.C.

Cheyenne

Famous tribe of Plains Indians. Allied with the Arapaho. Powerful, athletic, smart, brave. Horse Indians and buffalo hunters. Lived in tepees. Warlike—one of the most important tribes in the Indian conflicts on the Great Plains. The tribe was pushed into Nebraska by the Sioux. About 1832, the tribe split into the Northern and Southern Cheyenne. The Northern Cheyenne stayed in Nebraska. Placed in Indian Territory in 1876.

Confederacy

A union of different groups of people. A confederacy in Indian culture was a group of tribes that agreed not to fight with each other. They agreed to live peacefully. Sometimes the tribes shared culture and language.

Canoe

The Indians invented this useful boat. The "rough" side of the canoe was on the outside, not the inside!

Clan

A tribal unit. Members are descended from the same ancestor.

Citizenship

The Indian Citizenship Act of 1924 states all Indians born in the United States are citizens of the United States, and citizens of the states they live in, even though they may live on a reservation. They can vote. They pay most local, state and federal taxes, including sales taxes.

Cheyenne Outbreak

Bloodiest incident at Fort Robinson; Cheyenne chief Dull Knife led his tribe to seek shelter with Red Cloud. When they were held prisoner by the soldiers until they agreed to leave, they produced hidden weapons and killed 3 sentries to escape. The battle that followed ended with the death of 64 Indians.

Calumet

Also called "peace pipe" or "war pipe." Refers to the stem of the pipe, which is decorated with feathers or carved to signal the tribe's intentions. Nebraska Indians believed the calumet to have great power.

D is for . . .

Descendants

The first Nebraska Indians were descendants of primitive hunters who crossed the Bering Strait from Asia to what is now Alaska. At that time, glacial ice still covered most of North America. These people were the true discoverers of the "New World!"

Dance

There were Indian dances for every occasion: war, peace, hunting, rain, good harvests, etc. Drums, rattles, and flutes of bone or reed provided the music. Dancers often chanted or sang while performing. Steps were not easy to learn and required consistent practice.

Disease

Nebraska Indians had no immunity to the diseases that white explorers, colonists and settlers brought to their lands. These diseases included smallpox, measles, tuberculosis and others, which ravaged the tribes in great epidemics that killed many, and sometimes all, members of a tribe.

Dramatic Hair!

The Sac (Sauk) and Fox tribes were known for their big tuft of deer hair dyed red worn atop their head, which they had shaven bare!

Dyes

Made of lichens, berries, roots, bark, plants, and other natural materials by Indians in Nebraska. Different colors were used depending on what materials were available and what objects were to be dyed.

Decisions, Decisions!

The Cheyenne had a special council - the Council of Forty-four. Each of the 44 Cheyenne bands had a peace chief, who was on the council. They settled disputes, decided when to move, made tribal war policy decisions and decisions on alliances with other tribes.

Dishes

Made from clay, bark, wood, stone, and other materials, depending on what was available and what food they would be used for.

Dreams

Important in the Indian tradition. It was believed that dreams were the "windows" to the soul. Many thought a person's hidden desires were expressed in dreams.

E is for . . .

Eagle

An animal used in many Indian ceremonies. Eagle feathers attached to war bonnets and shields communicated an Indian's rank in his tribe and what kinds of deeds he had done. Feathers also adorned rattles, pipes, baskets, and prayer sticks.

Effigy Mound Culture

Built earthen figures of birds, animals or people.

Early Explorers

When the first explorers reached Nebraska in the early 1700s many Indian tribes lived here including the Arapaho, Cheyenne, Missouri, Omaha, Otoe, Pawnee, Ponca and Sioux. The Pawnee was the largest group.

Even Today!

These Indians tribes are located in Nebraska today: Iowa, Omaha, Ponca, Sac and Fox, Santee Sioux and Winnebago.

Earrings

Medicine men sometimes pierced male and female ears at special ceremonies. Earrings, which cost parents or relatives a significant amount, symbolized wealth and distinction. The more earrings that an Indian wore, the greater his honor. Some earrings measured 12 inches in length!

Environment

Preserving the environment is important to preserving Native American heritage. For thousands of years, Native American tribes lived completely off the land. Farming, mining, pollution have all had a part in changing native environments.

English

In the 1800s, the U.S. government built boarding schools for Indian children throughout the nation. Children were forced to leave their homes and families to live at these schools. They were required to learn English and not speak their native languages.

Epidemics

Few Indians possessed immunity to the deadly diseases, like smallpox and measles, which European explorers and settlers brought to the New World. As a result, great population loss took place. Sometimes entire tribes became extinct. Epidemics sparked by Hernando De Soto's expedition are estimated to have killed 75% of the native population in the New World.

F is for . . .

Fetish

These small objects were thought to hold the spirit of an animal or a part of nature. A fetish could be an object found in nature, such as bone or wood, or it could be a carved object. The fetish was usually small enough to be carried in a small bag or on a cord. The making and use of a fetish was kept secret by its owner and only shared with the one who inherited it.

Fort Omaha

Built in 1868 to protect the settlers, railroad and telegraph during the Indian Wars. Ponca chief Standing Bear's right to travel off of reservation land was successfully argued in a trial here. This recognized Indians as "persons" under the law for the first time in U.S. history.

Folsom Culture

Early peoples in Nebraska. Used stone knives and spear or arrow tips.

Fire Drill

A device used by Indians to make fires which consisted of a stick and a piece of wood with a tight hole in it. The stick was twirled rapidly in the hole, creating friction that would ignite shredded grass or wood powder placed nearby to start a fire.

Farmers

Many Nebraska Indians, ancient and modern, have farming ways! Even pre-contact Indians tilled and irrigated, raising many important crops. Corn, cotton, beans, squash, melons, sunflowers, gourds, pumpkins and tobacco are all native Indian crops!

Federal Recognition

The United States government's official acknowledgement of a group of Indians as a tribe that is eligible for government benefits, programs and funds.

Footwear

Nebraska Indians wore different footwear depending on their tribe and environment. Moccasins were made mostly of animal skin. Sandals were made of rawhide or plant material.

Fox

The native name for the tribe is "Mesquaki", meaning "red earth people". They were seminomadic. Raised crops in the summer, but hunted on the trail in the winter. Had three kinds of leaders—the peace chief, the war chief, and the ceremonial leader. Formed an alliance with the Sac (Sauk) in 1734 that continues today.

G is for . . .

Gens

Group of related members from different tribes.

Games

Adults played ball and other games of chance or skill. Indian children spun tops, fought pretend battles, did target-shooting, walked on stilts, played hide and seek, or competed to see who could hold their breath the longest!

Gathering

Native Americans gathered natural materials for food, fuel, baskets, clothing, and housing. American Indians tribes also hunted to meet basic needs. Even though some tribes planted crops, most did some kind of gathering.

Gorgets

Beautiful ornaments hung around the neck or from ears; their significance, if any, is unknown.

Go To These Exciting Indian Places in Our State

Annual Fort Robinson Intertribal Gathering – June, Crawford; Isanti Annual Traditional Wacipi – June, Santee; Annual Homecoming Celebration Winnebago Pow-Wow – July, Winnebago; Annual Ponca Pow Wow – August, Niobrara; Annual Omaha Pow Wow – August, Macy; Massacre Canyon Powwow – August, Trenton; Annual Omanisa Wacipi – October, North Platte.

Gourds

Hollowed-out shell of a gourd plant's dried fruit which often grew into a specific shape. Indians raised many species of gourds. They were used for spoons, bowls, masks, rattles, and even storage.

H is for . . .

Horn and Hooves

Indians used animal horn to make spoons and dishes. Hooves were made into rattles and bird beaks were used for decoration.

Hatchet

A small, short-handled ax, primarily used as a tool, not as a weapon. When settlers moved in, stone hatchets were replaced with iron ones.

Hair

Indians used hair as a textile. Hair from bison, mountain sheep, elk, moose, deer, dog, rabbit, beaver, or even humans were used to weave cloth, make wigs, or stuff pillows, balls, dolls or drumsticks.

Heritage House Museum

Weeping Water; see a prehistoric Indian artifact collection with items that date back thousands of years.

Horses

Spaniards brought the horse to America. At first, Indians were afraid of the horse or thought it was sacred. Later, Indians "broke" horses gently, often "hypnotizing" them with a blanket. Horses were used for transportation, trade, barter or payment. Some Indians ate horse meat in hopes of gaining the animal's power.

Hunters

Early Indian peoples were hunters who used wooden spears with stone points to kill many kinds of large mammals that are extinct today, such as mammoths and mastodons!

Hastings Museum

Hastings; collection of Sioux Indian artifacts and gallery of Plains Indian life.

Horse Creek Treaty

1851; officially known as the first Fort Laramie Treaty. The meeting, mean to be at Ft. Laramie, was moved to Horse Creek because of the number of attendees. Between 8,000 and 12,000 Indians from different tribes were there! The tribes signing were the Sioux, Cheyenne, Arapaho, Crow, Assinibone, Gros Ventre, Mandan, and the Arikara. The treaty called for no warfare and lasting peace between the tribes. It gave the U.S. the right to build roads and forts in the tribes' territories. It promised that the United States would protect the Indians from any "depredations" by its citizens. The U.S., for damages in the past and the future, was to pay $50,000 per year for 50 years (which Congress later cut to 10 years) to the nations in food, goods, livestock, and farming equipment. Safe passage for western-bound settlers from the Indians was also part of the treaty.

I is for . . .

Indian Removal Act of 1830

This federal act gave President Andrew Jackson the power to relocate tribes east of the Mississippi to an "Indian Territory." The forced removal of the southeast Indians later became known as the "Trail of Tears."

Indian Scout

This term for a guide applied to Indians or white-skinned people who served that role.

Indian Reservation

A tract of land set aside by a government for Indians to live on.

Independence

Native American tribes are sovereign nations. That means they are independent. Some even issue their own passports! However, Native Americans are also considered citizens of the United States and enjoy all the rights and privileges of U.S. citizens.

Ioway

Tribe also called the Iowa. Legend says they are descended from the Winnebago. Lived in Nebraska for a time before returning to Iowa. After ceding their lands, they were assigned to a reservation in 1836. Part of that land was in present-day Nebraska. Although smaller, the remainder of this reservation is in Richardson County and Brown County, Kansas.

Indian

In 1493, Christopher Columbus called the native people he met in North America "Indians" because he mistakenly believed he had sailed to India! Today, this term includes the aborigines of North and South America.

Indian Ladder

Indians made ladders by trimming branches off a tree. Some were left at consistent intervals to provide steps.

Indian Tribes in Nebraska

At one time or another, these tribes have lived in the state of Nebraska: Cheyenne, Ioway, Kaw, Kiowa, Missouria, Omaha, Otoe, Pawnee, Ponca, Sac, Fox, Winnebago

J is for . . .

Just So You Know . . .

Today you can find many Nebraska Indians that follow some traditional ways. But there are also many who are entrepreneurs, doctors, lawyers, educators and even politicians! If you visit a reservation or cultural event, make sure you know visitor etiquette. Often dances are religious ceremonies and should be observed as such; religious dances should not be applauded. Photography, videotaping and drawing are all important issues - check with the tribe or individual before any is started.

Jesuits

Roman Catholic priests called Jesuits were among the first to meet and live with the North American Indians. Their writings, sent back to Europe, serve as one of today's best references to early Indian life.

Justice?

For hundreds of years, Native Americans have not received justice from federal and state governments. Native Americans have had nearly all their land taken away. Native Americans still have to fight for their rights in courts across the land.

Judicial Termination

Modern term to describe current efforts by various U.S. government agencies and officials (especially the judicial system) to legally decrease the sovereignty of independent Indian tribes.

Just In Time!

The Indian Arts and Crafts Act of 1990 makes it against the law to pretend that an item has been made by Native Americans if it is really not. It is illegal to offer or display for sale, or sell any art or craft product in a way that falsely suggests it is Indian produced.

Jerked Meat

Thin strips of buffalo, elk, deer or other animal meat which is dried on racks in the sun; also called "jerky."

K is for . . .

Kaw

This tribe was also known as the Kansa. Kaw territory extended into southern Nebraska. Due to their distinct hairstyle of a shaved head with a single lock at the back, they were easily recognized. Their lands were reduced, exchanged, and almost all lost through the relocation of other tribes, settlement, and allotment.

Kill Site

An archaeological site where remains of many animals have been found along with human artifacts. Many kill sites have been useful to scientists in learning how ancient American Indians lived.

Killed Pottery

Pottery placed in a grave as an offering to the dead person was called killed pottery. A hole was formed in its base during creation. Often broken pottery was placed in a grave because Indians believed the spirit of the dead person would then be released and could travel.

Knife

Made from various materials such as bone, reed, stone, wood, antler, shell, metal, or animal teeth (bear, beaver, etc.), knives were used as weapons but also creative handiwork.

Kiowa

Warlike Indian tribe who were horse Indians and buffalo hunters. Among the most fierce warriors of America's Indians. Migrated several times, and noted by Lewis and Clark to be living along the North Platte River in the early 1800s.

Knots

Tied on bowstrings, spearhead and arrowhead lashings, snowshoes, and other items, knots were sometimes used to keep track of the days like a calendar—each knot equaled 1 day.

L is for . . .

Linguistic Families

There are 56 related groups of American Indian languages. A few of these speech families include Iroquoian, Algonquian, Siouan, Muskogean, Athapascan, and Wakashan.

Lower Loup

Peoples who were probably the ancestors of the Pawnee Indians.

Lost Tribes of Israel

This historic theory has been floating around since 721 BC. The 10 lost tribes of Israel are supposedly groups of people gathered together by Sargon, the King of Assyria. Some say he cast out 10 of the 12 tribes of Israel. Many have tried to prove that the American Indians are these missing tribes!

Leggings

Both men and women wore cloth or skin covering, which were often decorated with quills, beads, or painted designs, for their legs.

Lodge

The term for a type of Indian house that was usually a permanent dwelling. The population of a tribe was often estimated by its number of lodges.

Land Loss

Native Americans lost their land in many ways. Conflicts with other tribes, colonization, European settlement, treaties, and removal took away Indian lands.

Lance

Spear used for hunting and war. The hunting lance had a short shaft and a broad, heavy head. The war lance was light and had a long shaft.

"Lost the Corn":

Cheyenne expression from a legend that describes the Indians losing their settled agricultural way of life to Plains hunting, once they got the horse.

Lariat

These throw ropes made of rawhide, buffalo hair, or horsehair sometimes measured up to 20 feet long!

M is for . . .

Missouria

This tribe was encountered by Lewis and Clark south of the Platte River in Nebraska in the early 1800s. Osage attacks later moved them from here. Lived in villages and farmed until acquiring the horse.

Massacre Canyon

On the Republican River near Trenton. In 1873, a large party of Sioux ambushed a hunting party of Pawnee, including women and children. One of the last great intertribal confrontations in North America. A monument marks the site, and it was the last clash between the Sioux and Pawnee. Chief Sky Chief, a Pawnee known for providing scouts to the Army, was killed here with 150 of his people.

Maize

Also called Indian Corn. Known as a "cereal" plant because it probably began as some form of grass. The Indians in our state figured out every possible way to use corn as a food. The only thing the white man added was the creation of "corn flakes!"

Museum of Nebraska History

Lincoln; see "The First Nebraskans" exhibit, Plains Indian archaeology, a Pawnee earthlodge, Winnebago Reservation house and many photographs.

Moccasins

Indian shoes made of animal skin.

Medicine Man

A person who got the power to heal the sick through a secret means, usually from a dream or visions.

Mound Builders

About 2,000 years ago a wave of migrating people came to our area. They were the first of many groups to be known as the Mound Builders, for the earthenworks they created. Sometimes built high earthen walls around their villages, possibly for defense. They vanished long before the first white explorers reached Nebraska.

N is for . . .

Nomadic

The Sioux, Arapahoe and Cheyenne were nomadic hunters who roamed the plains of western Nebraska hunting buffalo. They built no permanent villages. They gathered vegetation instead of growing crops. They depended on the buffalo for food and clothing. They did not make pottery, but did decorate animal skins with beautiful and complex geometric designs.

Nebraska

The state is named for the word Otoe Indians and many whites used for the Platte River. Means "flat water."

Nation

There are many Indian nations located within the United States, such as the Winnebago Nation. Indian nations are called nations because their governments and laws are independent of and separate from the U.S. government. The federal government must have "government to government" relations with these Indian nations, just as it would with foreign nations, like England or Spain.

November

In 1990, President George Bush approved a joint resolution designating November 1990 "National American Indian Heritage Month." Similar proclamations have been issued each year since 1994.

Names

Indian names were often changed during one's lifetime. These names could be derived from events that happened during the person's birth, childhood, adolescence, war service, or retirement from active tribal life. Some names came from dreams, some were inherited, and sometimes names were stolen or taken in revenge. Today some Indians maintain old, traditional Indian names, while others take modern names. Since settlers often did not read or write Indian languages, they recorded Indian names phonetically (as they "sounded"). Thus Indian names were often misspelled.

National Museum of the American Indian

The Smithsonian's National Museum of the American Indian on the National Mall in Washington, D.C., symbolizes a deeper understanding between America's first citizens and those who have come to make these shores their home.

Nebraska Culture

Early native peoples who lived on the Missouri River. Lived in villages of 50-100 people. Used planting sticks to dig holes to plant corn and the shoulder bones of bison as hoes. Stored extra food in underground storage pits. Also hunted bison.

O is for . . .

Old Bones

No one knows for sure when the first people came to North America, but scientists have dated bones and artifacts discovered at Clovis, New Mexico around 11,200 years old. Testing on a skeleton found on the Channel Islands, off the coast of California showed they were about 13,000 years old. And, evidence of human habitation in southern New Mexico suggests that people may have been there as far back as 38,000 years ago.

Otoe

Ancestral relatives of the Missouria and the Ioway. After splitting from them, they settled in southeastern Nebraska. Pressured into giving away their lands in the 1830s.

Origins

Some scientists believe that Native Americans actually came across a land bridge between Asia and North America. They say that during an ice age thousands of years ago, the water level was much lower and people could have walked between the two continents.

Omaha

Gave their name to Nebraska's largest city. Lived in permanent villages between the Platte, Niobrara and Missouri rivers. Built large earth-lodges and cultivated crops. Carried the portable tepee with them when they went buffalo hunting. Known for their complex social structure. Ceded their lands in 1854 and granted a reservation.

Oil

Indians extracted oil from the many layers of fat that came with fresh bear meat. The fat was boiled down in earthen pots to produce the oil, which was stored in gourds and pots. The oil was used for cooking and even beautifying the body! Indians would mix red pigment with the oil, add the fragrances of cinnamon and sassafras, and rub it all over their bodies.

Orators

Many Indian leaders were excellent public speakers. Powerful and dramatic speakers were vital to leaders who wanted to influence their tribe. Watch for famous Indian quotations in literature and textbooks!

Office of Indian Education Programs

This is a service organization devoted to providing quality education opportunities for American Indian people. Established in the latter part of the nineteenth century to carry out the federal government's education commitment to Indian tribes, it has become the only national education system for American Indian children and adults.

P is for . . .

Powwow

The original form of the word meant "medicine man." Medicine men would often use noise motion and confusion to scare away harmful spirits and cure people. It was also a gathering to talk about political matters. Today, the powwow is an event where Indians gather to sing, perform ceremonial dances, and share cultural pride and traditions.

Ponca

Lived in northwest Nebraska along the mouth of the Niobrara River, spilling over into South Dakota. After being relocated, there was a famous incident that involved the funeral procession back to Nebraska to bury the dead son of Chief Standing Bear. Settlers seeing them pass let the Army know of a possible Indian uprising. The Indians reached Nebraska, only to be arrested. Support for them grew after some whites learned about the reason for their trip back to the homeland. With the help of sympathetic lawyers, a trial took place in 1879. The judge ruled in favor of the Indians, saying they had inalienable rights and the government could not by force keep them from returning to their homelands. Then they regained a reservation along the Niobrara in 1880. More importantly, the court set a precedent that showed Native Americans were equal under the law.

Pawnee

The Skidi band of this tribe lived along the Platte, Republican and Loup rivers. Sometimes called the Northern Pawnee. They came to Nebraska from the south and east. They built large, earth-covered lodges along riverbanks, grew corn, squash and beans. Frequently left their villages to hunt buffalo, taking cone-shaped, animal-skin tepees with them. Friendly to white settlers; famous as scouts for the U.S. Army in the 1860s to the 1880s. Gave up their lands in the mid 1800s for a reservation near Fullerton; that was lost in 1876.

Pemmican

Indian food made of animal meat, which was dried in the sun, pounded together with fat and berries. The mixture was packed into skin bags and used primarily while on the trail.

Paint

Indians used many natural materials to make paint, like clay mixed with oil or grease. Yellow "paint" was made with the gall bladder of a buffalo! Why did they paint their faces or bodies? Indians used paint to look scary or beautiful, to disguise themselves, or to protect their skin from sunburn or insect bites. Indians often applied red paint because it symbolized strength and success.

Pine Ridge Reservation

Oglala Sioux. Located in South Dakota, with a small portion in Nebraska. 1,771,000 acres; more than 20,000 Indians live here.

Papoose

An American Indian infant aged between birth and one year is called a papoose. A papoose spent most of his or her days snugly wrapped in a kind of cradle made of skins or bark and a wooden frame that hung on the mother's back. This sturdy frame also allowed a mother to lean her papoose against a tree or rock within sight as she worked.

Pottery

Indian pottery was made from built-up spirals of clay that were molded or paddled, or a combination of the two methods. Most pottery served as cooking vessels.

Q is for . . .

Quillwork

Indians used the quills of porcupine or birds to make a type of embroidery. Quills were dyed with juice from berries and other materials. When they were ready to be used, the quills were either mashed with teeth or softened with hot water and flattened with rocks. The quills were then laced into moccasins, shirts, pipe covers, and other items. Beads which Indians received by trading with settlers eventually replaced quillwork.

Quality

Native American arts and crafts are known for their excellent craftsmanship and striking designs. This work is often influenced by things found in nature especially plants and animals.

Quiver

Case used to hold arrows; made of woven plant materials or animal skins.

Quarry Site

A location where Indians went for workable stone such as flint and made stone tools.

Quirt

A short riding whip with a wood, bone, or horn handle.

R is for . . .

Rain Dancing

The rain dance ceremony, performed to encourage rainfall, was common among Indian religions because good weather is vital for a successful harvest. Rainmakers were in tune with nature; there are actual reported cases of Indians producing or preventing rain!

Roots

Indians used plant roots for food, medicine, dye, baskets, cloth, rope, salt, flavoring, and just to chew!

Rattles

Indians of Nebraska made rattles from bird beaks, animal hooves, bones, pods, seashells, turtle shells and other animal parts. The rattles are used in ceremonies.

Railroad Woes

Indians in western Nebraska soon realized that the iron rails threatened their nomadic way of life. A series of uprisings began in 1864 in the Platte Valley. Indian tribes cooperated to fight the completion of rail lines across the state. Indians attacked stagecoaches, tore down telegraph wires and ripped up track.

Rawhide

Untanned animal hide. The "green" hide was stretched on the ground or over a frame. Flesh and fat were removed. The skin was dried, washed, then buried with wood ashes which made the hair come off. Used by the Nebraska Indian to make drumheads, lash lodge poles, mend broken objects and in many other ways.

Removal

The U.S. government policy of the 1830s-1850s that removed Indians from their native lands to new lands, primarily west of the Mississippi River.

Reservations

The U.S. government set aside, or "reserved," land for the Indians. These reservations originally served as a sort of prison during the beginning stages of Indian removal. At that time, reservations provided the government with some control over Indian activity and residency. This land was usually considerably less desirable land than the Indians' native territories. Today's reservations are lands that are tribally held, yet protected by the government.

River Indians

The Ponca, Otoe, Omaha and Missouri Indians lived along the riverbanks, mostly in eastern Nebraska.

S is for . . .

Secret Societies

Indians had secret groups, usually organized for religious or ceremonial reasons. Each society had a purpose, such as to cure disease.

Scotts Bluff

The Plains Indians called this enormous ship-shaped rock Me-a-pa-te, "the hill that is hard to go around."

Shaman

Medicine man and spiritual leader who was supposed to have special healing power from another world.

Shield

A piece of "armor" made of a rawhide-covered frame, which was carried into battle. Shields also could be decorative and religious objects. Many tribes make shields today as an art form!

Sweatlodge

Structure used for ritual purification by sweating from exposure to very hot fires or hot steam from pouring water over hot stones. Also called a sweathouse, for some tribes also doubling as clubhouses.

Sioux

These Indians considered themselves superior to their Pawnee neighbors. The western Sioux were part of a large confederation of tribes that lived from the Great Lakes to the Dakotas. They sometimes used the plains of western Nebraska as hunting grounds.

Sacred Bundles

A group of objects treasured by a tribe. They were well-guarded and often taken into battle. The items were publicly shown only on very important occasions.

Santee Sioux Reservation

Niobrara; 504 Indians on 9,358 acres. Located on the shores of Lewis and Clark Lake, established in 1863.

Stone-boiling

Cooking method by placing preheated stones into cooking vessels.

Sac

Tribe of Indians, also known as the Sauk. Closely allied with the Fox. Originally woodland Indians that farmed in villages during the warm seasons and roamed hunting in the cold seasons. Migrated often. Lost their lands and were relocated. Today, their descendants can be found in the Sac and Fox Tribe of Missouri, located in Nebraska and Kansas.

Signal Butte

Site of an early Nebraska Indian culture. Excavations show they were hunters who had little or no agriculture.

Shun-ka wakan

Means "sacred dogs;" what the Sioux called their horses.

T is for . . .

Tobacco

A sacred plant early Indians used to make offering to their gods, cure diseases, bring good luck, seal agreements and bind treaties.

Totem

The spirit of some natural object (usually an animal) taken by an Indian, tribe or family to guard over them.

Tracking

To follow a trail by finding a sign such as a broken blade of grass, a moved stone or moccasin track. Indians learned to trail as children, so that they could find food, track enemies and disguise their own signs.

"Talking Wires"

What the Indians called the telegraph poles that went up across the state. When they realized that soldiers followed the lines, they set the poles on fire and attacked telegraph stations along the "Great Medicine Road" on fire.

Treaties

Written agreements between the U.S. government and the Indians, most of which involved the Indians giving up their native lands. A series of treaties between the United States and the Indians in the 1830s to the 1860s reduced the Indians' claims to the vast lands of Nebraska. While many of the Indian tribes in eastern Nebraska had ceded their lands to the government by the time the Nebraska Territory was formed, Indians in the western part of the state continued to fight against white encroachment.

Tribe

A group of Indians with shared culture, history, original territory, ancestry, social organization, and governmental structure. A tribe may contain several bands of Indians.

Throwing Stick

A sling or grooved stick used to hurl a lance or spear. It was used by Nebraska Indians before bows and arrows.

Tomahawk

A club, axe or hammer used to chop wood, drive stakes in the ground or as a weapon.

Teeth

Nebraska Indians hung teeth on cords to make necklaces.

Thunderbird

A mythological Indian figure, as well as a part of the constellations for many Indians. Thunderbird mythology is mostly different from tribe to tribe, in general either coexisting with ancestors as an actual bird, or appearing as a spiritual nature god. The Thunderbird was good to the people in either case. Much mythology ties the thunderbird with thunder, lightning and storms.

U is for . . .

U.S. Bureau of Indian Affairs

Provides public services such as law enforcement, land records, economic development, and education to Indians. Known for mismanagement and ethical problems.

U. S. Indian Territory

This former "territory" is now part of the United States. It contained parts of what today is Nebraska, Colorado and Wyoming, and all of Kansas and Oklahoma. Never made official by Congress, Indians were removed to the "territory" anyway. Indians living here had their lands greatly reduced to accommodate relocated tribes, starting in the 1830s. Over the next 40 years, the "territory" got smaller and smaller until only a portion of Oklahoma remained.

U.S. Indian Reorganization Act

Passed by Congress in 1934, the act authorized Indian tribes to establish and conduct their own governments, and to form businesses.

Understanding the Indians

Many misconceptions still survive about the American Indians of the Great Plains. Contrary to what some television shows and movies depict, they seldom attacked the wagon trains of settlers traipsing across Nebraska. It was only after the Indians realized that so very many settlers were coming and intended to take over virtually all the Indian land they possibly could, that some tribes retaliated by battling to keep their traditional hunting grounds and homelands.

Upper Republican Culture

Early peoples who lived along the banks of the Republican River in southern Nebraska and on the Loup River in the central part of the state. Lived in villages, grew crops, stored food for winter and hunted bison.

U.S. Indian Wars

The U.S. War Department has compiled an official list of "Indian Wars" that occurred in the United States. Over 50 wars were fought between the U.S. and the Indians during the period of 1790-1850.

U.S. Indian Schools

The Bureau of Indian Affairs operates hundreds of federal schools around the nation. Enrollment of Native American children measures in the thousands!

V is for . . .

Vessels

Indians carried water in special gourds shaped liked bottles, called water vessels.

Village Councils

These were held in the town (council) house and occurred to discuss and decide important matters. Harmony and agreement was essential to tribal unity. Rather than vote on issues, they were discussed until everyone was satisfied. Anyone who wanted to could speak freely. Everyone did not always agree on the outcome, but everyone avoided conflict by pushing their case.

Vegetable Dyes

Indians could not buy color from the store like we can today. Instead, they created many different colors from the things they found on earth like plants, flowers, shrubs, trees, roots, and berries. They made beautiful and unique reds, oranges, yellows, greens, browns, and violets. These dyes were used for baskets, pottery, weaving, body makeup, and clothing.

Very Hungry

There were Indians who here hunters, gatherers and foragers, that often ate whatever they could find! How hungry would you have to be to eat what they sometimes ate: reptiles, larvae, and insects?

Villages

Many Nebraska Indians lived in villages! Villages were formed around different clans or bands within the tribe, but could also contain different clans living together. Villages were usually permanent settlements, although semi-nomadic tribes have been known to migrate between permanent villages.

Vesperic Indians

Indian tribes located in the United States.

W is for . . .

War Bonnet

Special headdress worn into battle, often adorned with feathers.

War Pony

Horse, often painted with colorful paint and ridden into battle.

Winnebago Reservation

Located in Thurston County. 1,154 Indians on 27,537 acres in Nebraska with portions in Iowa. Bordered by the Missouri River and the Omaha Reservation.

War Dance

Indian braves danced this before going into battle. The dance was a way of assembling the braves and getting them to commit to the fight ahead.

Winnebago

This central Great Lakes woodland tribe lived in villages of rectangular bark lodges, but also went on the trail to hunt buffalo. They hunted, fished, gathered and farmed for their food. The "Winnebago Way" means to live with a reverence for nature. After the Black Hawk War, they were relocated four times. The fourth time brought them to Nebraska, where their descendants can be found today.

Whistle

Indians from Nebraska made them from the wing bones of birds. The whistles made the sound of the bird the bones came from! Used to communicate, signal, sound an alarm or even flirt with a maiden!

War Club

A weapon made of stone, bone, or wood in the shape of a club.

White Man

Indians generally called them Pale Face, a name the white men themselves suggested!

Woodland Period

The first known pottery in Nebraska dates from 100 B.C. to A.D. 900. These people made simple pottery, probably grew squash and gourds and were not as nomadic as some tribes. May have come here from the eastern part of America.

XYZ are for . . .

Xenophobe

A xenophobe is someone who is afraid of foreign people, their customs and cultures, or foreign things. Many of the first European settlers were afraid of Native American cultures.

You Bet!

Some Native Americans say that Casinos make a lot of money. Others say that too many people have a gambling problem. In the 1980s and 1990s, many tribes discussed whether or not gambling casinos should be allowed. Now that many casinos have been built across the country, the debate has switched to how it should be controlled.

Zounds!

Between 1871 and 1913, at least 98 traditional agreements between tribes and the United States were negotiated and 96 of them were ratified by Congress. Each agreement remains as law (unless changed by a later agreement)!

ZZZZZZ...

Shamans and medicine men were not the only people who had access to the spirit world. Indians believed that people could make contact with spirits every night in their dreams! Dreamers could travel back to the time of man's creation or far ahead into their own futures. They also believed that dreams contained warnings or commands from the spirits. Many tribes felt that they had to act out their dreams as soon as they awoke. If an Indian dreamed about bathing, for example, he would run to his neighbors' houses first thing in the morning, and his neighbors would throw kettles full of cold water over him.

Y... Or, "Why?"

1. Why do you think Indian warriors carried charms with them? Some Indian medicines have been scientifically proven to have true healing power and are still used today. Do you think their charms had any real power to help them win battles?
2. Why do you think the American government kept relocating Indians onto reservations and then making the reservations smaller and smaller?
3. Why did Indians use items such as a pipe in ceremonies? What kinds of symbolic objects do we use in ceremonies today?
4. Why and how did Indians use natural materials in creative ways?
5. Many Indian tribes are running successful businesses on their reservations today. There is one industry that many tribes are making a lot of money at. Do you know what this is? Hint: "I'll bet you do!"

Which Famous Native American Am I?

Solve the puzzle!

Word Bank

Black Elk	Crazy Horse	Sitting Bull	Sequoia
Sacajawea	Chief Joseph	Geronimo	Pocahontas

Down

1. This Shoshone woman joined Lewis and Clark as their guide and translator and helped make the expedition a success! Hint: She has 4 "a"s in her name!
4. This man gave the Cherokee their first alphabet so that they could write. Until then, they communicated only by speaking and drawing pictures. Hint: A famous ancient tree also has the same name!
5. He was one of the fiercest of Indian warriors! He fought against white settlers in Arizona and New Mexico to keep his people from being pushed off their lands. Hint: Jump!

Across

2. A legend says that this brave Algonquian woman saved the life of Englishman John Smith. Hint: Disney produced a movie about her.
3. He fought at Little Bighorn when he was only 13! He was also a wise "shaman" who saw visions and could advise people. Hint: Part of his name is an animal with antlers!
6. He was a great Sioux warrior who won the battle against General Custer at Little Bighorn in 1876. Hint: His horse was not crazy!
7. A leader of the Lakota (Sioux) tribe who lived on the Standing Rock Reservation in North Dakota after the battle of Little Bighorn. He tried to make conditions better for his people there, so the U.S. government called him a "troublemaker." Hint: He did not sit all the time!
8. A wise and brave chief of the Nez Percé who tried to bring his people to Canada to escape war. He said, "From where the sun now stands, I will fight no more forever." Hint: His father's name was "Old Joseph."

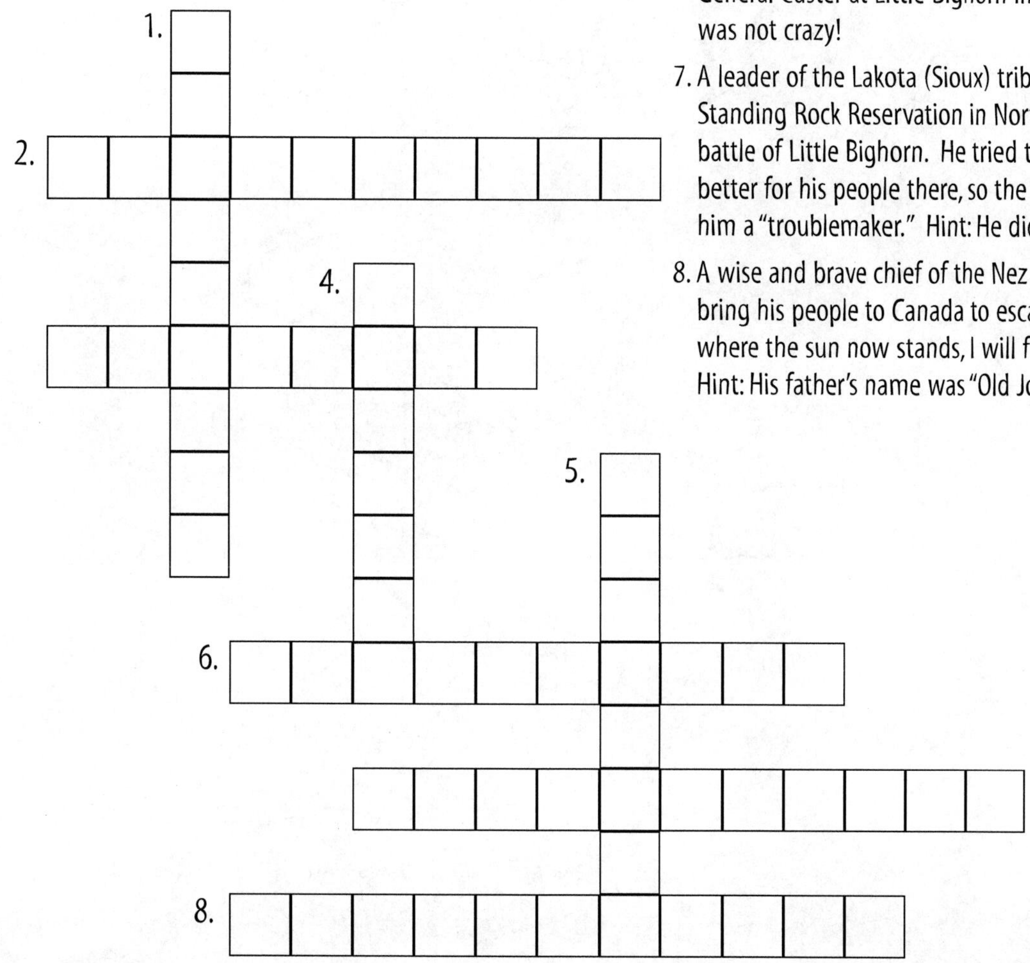

Answer Key: 1. Sacajawea; 2. Pocahontas; 3. Black Elk; 4. Sequoia; 5. Geronimo; 6. Crazy Horse; 7. Sitting Bull; 8. Chief Joseph

Different Ways for Different Indians!

North American Indian tribes are divided into different areas. In each of these areas, tribes shared common ways of living with each other. They might make similar arts or crafts, they might eat the same foods, or they might have had the same beliefs. These activities are all part of their "culture." Each area had its own culture, which was different from the tribes in all the other areas.

Below is a map of all the different groups of Indian tribes in North America. Color each area with a different color. You will see a colorful picture of how Native Americans can all be called "Indians" but still have very different cultures!

Celebration!

Powwows are big festivals where Native Americans gather to sing, dance, and eat together. It is a time to celebrate and show pride in their culture. Powwows can last from one afternoon to several days. The Indians dress in native costumes and dance ancient dances to the beating of drums.

Artists sell their arts and crafts. You might be able to buy some real Native American food cooked on an open fire. Native Americans go to powwows to be with each other, share ideas, and just have fun! Most powwows are also open to people who are not Indian. It's a great place to learn about Native American culture!

If you went to a powwow this weekend, what do you think you would see? What do you think might NOT be there? Circle the objects you think you would see at a powwow. Put an X through those you probably won't see.

Answer Key: Circled objects are: beads, moccasins, open fire, drums, feathers, baskets, kids, food, drums, horse.

Make an Indian Weaving!

Many Native Americans used weaving to create useful things like sashes (belts), bags, mats, and blankets. They used animal hair to make yarn, and dyed the yarn with natural dyes from fruits and other plants. They also used some plant fibers, like cotton, to make weaving thread.

Weave a small Native American mat of your own. Use different colors of yarn to create a beautiful pattern in your weaving. Place a favorite object on the mat or hang it on your wall!

Prepare the "loom"

Cut a piece of cardboard 5 inches wide and 6 inches long. Along the two 5-inch sides (the "short" sides), have an adult cut slits 1/4 inch deep. These slits should be 1/2 inch apart from each other. So, on each short side you will have 9 slits.

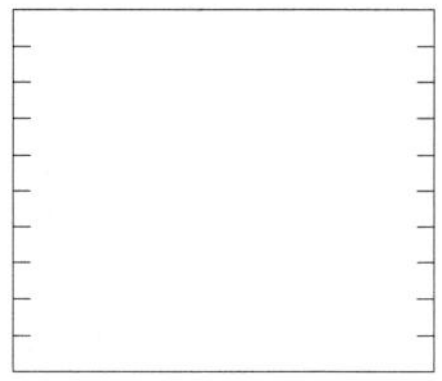

Directions:

1. Take a long piece of yarn and bring it from the back through the first slit (the one next to the edge of the cardboard.) The end of the yarn will hang down behind the cardboard.

2. Bring the yarn right across the front of the cardboard to the slit opposite the one your yarn came through.

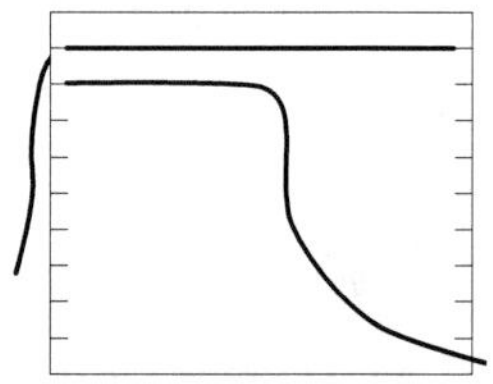

3. Now bring the yarn under the back of the cardboard and then up again through the second slit.

4. Repeat #2 and #3, until you have 9 strands of yarn across the front of your cardboard!

5. Then cut the yarn and tie the two loose ends in the back of the cardboard.

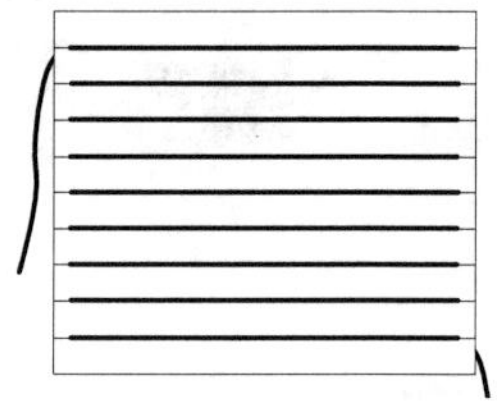

6. Take another piece of yarn and start feeding it through the 9 strands, going over one, under the next over the next, etc. When you get to the end, pull the yarn behind the cardboard and around to the front, and begin again. This time, whatever strand you went over, go under. And whatever strand you went under, go over.

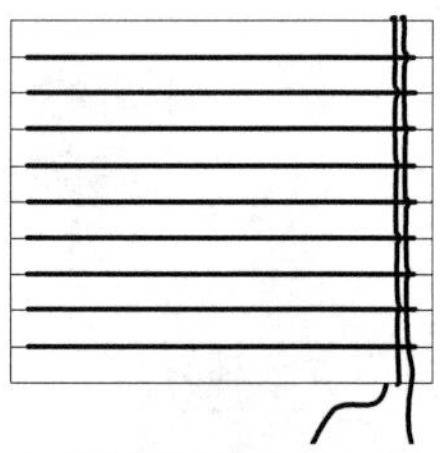

7. Repeat this pattern until the front of your cardboard in covered. Then cut the yarn in the back of the cardboard, and trim it to create a fringe for your mat!

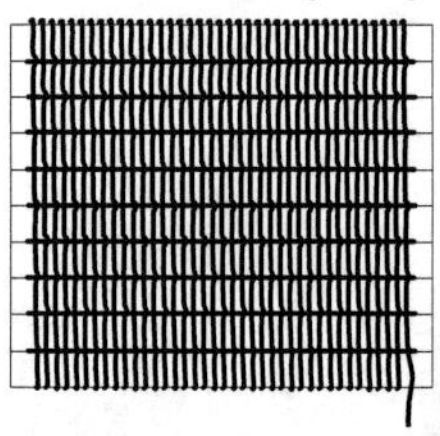

Tips:

- For a wild look, use variegated or different colored yarn!
- For a tighter mat, push the under/over strands up against the previous strands during weaving.
- To keep your mat from unravelling, tie neighboring fringe together up close to the mat.

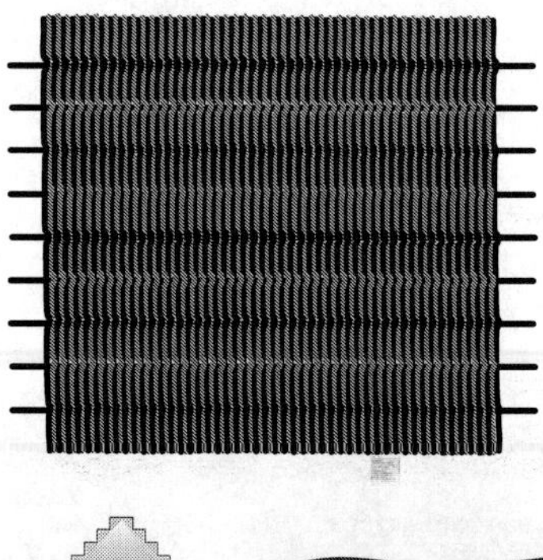

Finders Keepers?

Native Americans have many buried treasures. For hundreds of years, special objects would sometimes be buried with Native Americans, or maybe they would just be lost. Archeologists used to dig for interesting artifacts in old Native American gravesites. They would keep the Native American bones or the arrowheads, rattles, masks and other objects that they found. But this made the Native Americans feel like they were being robbed.

In 1990, the U.S. government passed a law that said that no one could look for or take these Native American objects anymore. And whoever had any already had to give them back to the people they belonged to. This is called repatriation

Help the archeologist return the artifact to a Native American.

Fast Fact

An artifact is an object that was made by people a long time ago for some useful purpose.

Busy Hands!

Before modern times, Native Americans didn't have stores where they went to buy things. They made everything they needed.

What did Indians make with their own hands? Use the Word Bank and pictures to find out!

Word Bank

blanket
moccasins

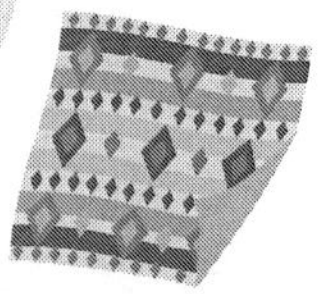 ___ ___ ___

 ___ ___ ___ ___

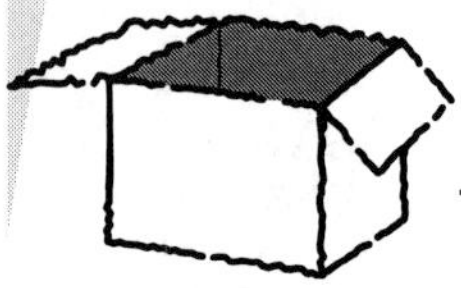 ___ ___ ___

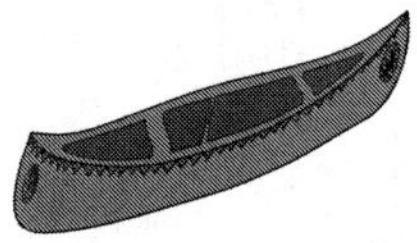 ___ ___ ___ ___ ___

 ___ ___ ___ ___ ___ ___ ___

 ___ ___ ___ ___ ___

 ___ ___ ___ ___ ___ ___ ___ ___ ___ ___ ___

 ___ ___ ___ ___ ___ ___

 ___ ___ ___ ___ ___ ___ ___

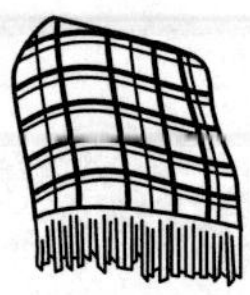 ___ ___ ___ ___ ___ ___ ___

American Indians Today

Beginning with the first letter of each group of letters, cross out every other letter to discover some new words. You may not have heard of these before, but you can read all about them!

1. Many Indians live on these, but many more do not!

TRYELSDEBRNVJAOTPIPOWNASX

____

2. Many Indians have been poor for a long time because for many years the government took away their lands and their ability to make a living.

TPKOOVWEBRNTXYA

____

3. Many Indians have been studying hard at school and going to college in order to earn more money. Education helps the Indians make their lives better. These Native Americans are working to become:

TSJUMCBCFEYSMSOFPUVL

____

4. This is a big term that means Native Americans have worked hard to get the U.S. government to let them rule themselves. This means that they have their own laws and make their own decisions. They are like a separate country inside the U.S.! Now, try and see if you can get your parents to give you the same thing!

TSGENLBF **JDGEETSEWRAMCIHNUAKTYIKOTNU**

______________ ______________________________

Fast Fact

What do Indians work as today?

- doctors
- nurses
- factory workers
- artists
- lawyers
- actors

The same kinds of jobs any American might work at!

Native Americans Move to the City!

Solve the code to discover the mystery words!

A	B	C	D	E	F	G	H	I	J	K	L	M
✹	❁	✣	♣	➳	❤	❢	✲	✄	✆	☛	✈	✉
N	**O**	**P**	**Q**	**R**	**S**	**T**	**U**	**V**	**W**	**X**	**Y**	**Z**
✿	✩	✦	✡	✐	❦	☎	✑	✙	✖	✍	✠	✓

1. During the 1950s and 1960s, the American government paid Indians to leave their homes on reservations and move to cities to get jobs. If cities are sometimes called urban areas, then these brave Indians were called:

___ ___ ___ ___ ___   ___ ___ ___ ___ ___ ___ ___

✑ ✐ ❁ ✹ ✿   ✄ ✿ ♣ ✄ ✹ ✿ ❦

2. Many Indians chose to stay on their reservations and not move to the city. They thought that if they moved to the city, they would lose the way of life that their parents and ancestors had taught. These Indians called themselves:

___ ___ ___ ___ ___ ___ ___ ___ ___ ___ ___   ___ ___ ___ ___ ___ ___ ___

✐ ➳ ❦ ➳ ✐ ✙ ✹ ☎ ✄ ✩ ✿   ✄ ✿ ♣ ✄ ✹ ✿ ❦

3. Native Americans who moved to cities lived close to each other. They tried to keep their way of life as much as possible. They did not want to forget their religion, native art, or music. They did not want to lose their:

___ ___ ___ ___ ___ ___ ___

✣ ✑ ✈ ☎ ✑ ✐ ➳

4. Are you afraid of heights? Many people are. The Mohawk Indians are not! Many of them work hundreds of feet above the city to build steel frames for skyscrapers. People who do this work above the city are:

___ ___ ___ ___ ___   ___ ___ ___ ___ ___ ___ ___

❦ ☎ ➳ ➳ ✈   ✖ ✩ ✐ ☛ ➳ ✐ ❦

5. Today urban Indians and reservation Indians come together to celebrate their culture. They share ideas and stories. They dance and beat drums. They make and sell Indian jewelry. During these celebrations, Indians remember how much they have to be proud of! These big parties are called

___ ___ ___ ___ ___ ___ ___

✦ ✩ ✖ ✖ ✩ ✖ ❦